Very Wicked Headmistress

ATE

THE ... MISS TAFFETA, notorious cheater and
black... ...er trapeze artist and human cannonball,
opens ... ...hool for rich young ladies. Everything
seems ... ...he school has never had so many teachers
and suc... ...ty of staff. However, when certain odd
things ... ...the girls begin to get a bit suspicious.
Is M... ...a connected with the mysterious volcanic
erupti... ...ustard or the discovery of diamonds within it?

*Another ... ...derful tale by the two time Carnegie Medal winner
Ma ga... ...hy.*

Other books by Margaret Mahy

THE RIDDLE OF THE FROZEN PHANTOM   *HarperCollins*

THE MAN WHOSE MOTHER WAS A PIRATE   *Puffin*

THE GREAT WHITE MAN-EATING SHARK   *Puffin*

A VILLAIN S NIGHT OUT   *Puffin*

SIMPLY DELICIOUS   *Frances Lincoln*

Margaret Mahy

The Very Wicked
Headmistress

ILLUSTRATED BY MARGARET CHAMBERLAIN

BARN OWL BOOKS

The Very Wicked Headmistress was first published
in 1984 by J. M. Dent & Sons Ltd
This edition published in 2005 by Barn Owl Books
157 Fortis Green Road, London N10 3LX
Barn Owl Books are distributed by Frances Lincoln
4 Torriano Mews, Torriano Avenue, London NW5 2RZ

ISBN 1-903015-46-4

Designed and typeset by Douglas Martin
Printed and bound by Imago in China

For Jake, Jesse and Jethro

[1]

A Very Wicked Headmistress

There was once a wicked headmistress called Miss Taffeta who ran a select school for girls. She had had a mixed but very adventurous career before she went in for education, beginning as an aerial trapeze artist and going on to considerable success as Consuela, the Human Cannonball. She thought nothing of being fired out of a cannon wearing a smile and a bikini and occasionally – when too much gunpowder was used – only a smile.

After some years of blackmailing and cheating at cards she found herself the owner of a fine old home many storeys high and so covered with ivy and fire-escapes that from a distance it looked like a huge model of snakes-and-ladders.

"I shall try running a girls' school," she said to her brother, who was just as wicked as she but, lacking her energy, seemed much better behaved.

"It would cost a fortune," he replied, lighting

7

an expensive cigar.

"Bainbridge," she exclaimed (for such was his name), "Bainbridge, I shall run this school at immense profit by making use of the fire-escapes, and my experience as a trapeze artist. Now take off that gorilla suit and dress as a butler, because the parents will be arriving soon."

Bainbridge had appeared with his sister in one particular circus as a dancing gorilla, and he had grown to love his gorilla suit. When he put it on his anxieties all left him like bad dreams.

"Tatiana, I am a gorilla at heart," he said, with a melancholy smile.

"You can wear it upstairs in the evening," she replied, and he had to be content with that.

[2]

A Farmer with an Unfortunate Weakness

Not far from the new school was a farm belonging to Mr Fendalton Bassett, a very susceptible man. Like Miss Taffeta, he had a mixed history. A man of many talents (he was a Doctor of Philosophy and could juggle three oranges with one hand) he had, nevertheless, a terrible weakness that had prevented him making the most of himself. He kept falling in love.

His was an affectionate nature, and even if a woman was very plain he could always find some bit of her he simply could not resist – an ankle, or her fingertips or even her left eyebrow. It had caused him a lot of trouble one way and another and he had decided, after his last sensational romance had been mentioned in the newspapers, to go into the country and live like a hermit, reading philosophy and keeping free-range hens.

He did not plan to live alone, however, for he

had adopted an orphaned nephew, Tancred, one of those freckled boys, shy but very reliable. Tancred's main job was supposed to be answering the door and the telephone in case the caller happened to be a woman and Fendalton's impulsive nature got out of hand and he fell in love again. As well as this, however, Tancred found himself doing most of the work on the farm while Fendalton stayed inside reading and sighing. Tancred took his duties very seriously, for his mother (Fendalton's sister) had been head prefect at her school and he had inherited her old school uniform and prefect's badge. It gave him a lot to live up to.

"You don't know what it is to be struck down by love," moaned Fendalton as Tancred made up buckets of hens' mash. "Yet how can I help it

when the world is brimful of absolutely fascinating women? It is a cruel thing to have to
limit yourself to one or two."

"Tough!" sympathized Tancred tersely.
"Lucky I'm here to help you, Uncle Fendalton. I
don't like girls much myself so I can be really
useful."

"Thank you," mumbled Fendalton, picking up
a heavy philosophy book, but looking very discontented as he did so.

[3]

The Staff of
Forest Glades School for Girls

The Forest Glades School for Girls did well
from the first day. The fees were so high that
people thought it simply must be worthwhile.
Rich parents turned up in shining cars driven
by haughty chauffeurs and were met at the door
by Bainbridge (dressed as a butler, of course,
not as a gorilla).

"Miss Taffeta's office is on the top floor," he
would tell them, conducting them to the lift
which had famous oil paintings all over its
walls, and, in one corner, a huge Greek statue,
draped in a Spanish shawl, so that people using
the lift were aware of classical art, geography
and modesty all in one go.

The lift set off, creeping up to the top of the
building, and Bainbridge would whip out his
walkie-talkie, and speak into it in an urgent
voice.

"Bainbridge calling Tatiana! Bainbridge call-

ing Tatiana! Come in, Tatiana."

"I read you loud and clear, Bainbridge. Come
in, Bainbridge," Miss Taffeta would say from
the top storey of the house.

"They're on their way up," Bainbridge would

report. "Two Rolls Royces and a Daimler."

"Roger!" Miss Taffeta would exclaim. "Take note, Bainbridge, no slipping into your gorilla suit until they're well clear of the school. Understood?"

"Understood!" Bainbridge would reply sadly.

"OK, over and out." Miss Taffeta's voice was always as crisp as a green apple.

She herself was dressed in a flowery dress, rather long, with her stormy black curls covered by an elegant grey wig. She would wipe off her lipstick and eye shadow and assume a calm, benevolent expression that always impressed the parents.

The lift was so weighted down with art that it travelled very slowly, though the parents did not notice this as there was so much to look at, and the Spanish shawl lent an air of mystery that intrigued them. But they were delighted to meet Miss Taffeta at last, sitting in her book-lined study, with a pile of perfectly neat exercise books set out in front of her, all marked with ticks and compliments. Little did the parents realize, as they listened to her understanding remarks, that she had been known to cheat at

cards, turn a double-somersault in mid-air without a net underneath her, and draw her gun (a
Colt *Peacemaker*) without the slightest hesitation.

"I'm glad we had this little talk," she would

say at last. "Now go down to the next floor
where you may speak with Mrs Function, our
mathematics teacher."

As the parents descended in the slow, but
cultured, lift Miss Taffeta was out of the study
window in a flash and down the fire-escape.
Taking off the grey wig, she replaced it with a

stern, brown one. She put on stern, flat shoes, and stern steel-rimmed spectacles while she was over a hundred feet above the school playground. When the parents met her on the next floor they did not recognize her, or on the next floor, or on the floor after that. In this way Miss Taffeta appeared not only as Mrs Function, the mathematics teacher, but as Madame le Sage, the French teacher, Miss Wordsworth, the English teacher, Dr Anne Wheeze, the old science and technology teacher, not to mention Matron Casubon, and the cook, Mrs Wheatley. Miss Taffeta enjoyed all these parts, and almost came to believe she actually was in charge of a large and efficient staff. Even Bainbridge had two parts to play – appearing both as the school butler and as an old, but lovable, caretaker called Wetwax. However he hated being either of them, particularly Wetwax, whose job it was to look after the school boiler which was very old and, like a bent trombone, had a lot of trouble with valves.

Nevertheless, it was easy to see that the parents driving out through the school gates were very much impressed with what they had seen,

and thought it was hardly surprising that such
a well-staffed school, with such an artistic lift,
should be a little on the expensive side. They
could not guess that the staff consisted of only
two people, two people such as one would hardly wish to entrust with the education of sixty
growing girls, all as sensitive and artistic as
only the children of rich people can afford to be.

4

An Explosive Event on Fendalton's Farm

Meanwhile, things were going rather badly on the farm. It was what is called a mixed farm – fields of sugarbeet, a flock of free-range hens and a herd of Friesian cows whose milk was stored in a large refrigerated tank until the dairy factory came with tankers to take it away. It should have been easy for two people to man-age such a productive unit. However, after the first week, Fendalton began sneezing and claimed to be allergic to feathers, milk and newly turned earth, so he stayed indoors read-ing philosophy while Tancred fed the free-range hens and milked the cows. He enjoyed the work and did it very well, talking to the cows and hens in a reassuring way, and even to the sugar-beet as he weeded around it, but do what he could, things began to get beyond him. The milk tank leaked, and the free-range hens made their nests among the sugarbeet and hid their eggs so well they were very hard to find. It was a lot of responsibility for one boy – even one whose mother had been a head prefect.

However, the worst thing was that the farm was the scene of volcanic activity. There were warm pools (delightful for swimming in), and boiling pools (useful for making tea and cooking eggs for breakfast), but on the whole, what with the geysers and the hot mud, the volcanic side of things was more trouble than it was worth. And then one night a volcano actually blew up in the very middle of the sugarbeet fields. It was small but powerful. Tancred and Fendalton spent a fretful night crouched under the table which was very strong. By morning the volcano had quietened down again leaving a crater among the sugarbeet and an atmosphere of strange desolation over the rest of the farm. The cows and hens had run away to safer farms in the area, the milk tank was split in half and the milk had run away, too. Meanwhile, around the crater a huge mountain had gradually formed, made of a mysterious, oozing, yellow substance that completely covered what was left of the sugarbeet.

"Oh joy!" cried Fendalton. He was already tired

of farming and philosophy, and had begun to think that he could face the risks of beautiful women with fortitude once more.

"I shall be able to claim on the insurance now and move out of the volcanic zone," he cried.

"What *is* that yellow stuff?" Tancred wondered.

"Oh, just lava, I suppose," Fendalton said airily. "Lava or a new variety of mud. I'm insured against both." He was already planning to spend the insurance money on a refreshing cruise among the Pacific islands.

But Tancred sniffed the yellow mountain, and then bravely tasted it.

"Uncle Fendalton," he cried, "this isn't mud. It's custard – caramel custard!"

"Caramel custard!" groaned Fendalton, suddenly aghast.

"It's very strange," Tancred replied, "but, Uncle, I see what must have happened. The milk ran into the sugarbeet and the free-range eggs, and the volcano has mixed them all together, and cooked them into the biggest caramel custard in the world. It must be a million to one chance of a thing like that happening."

Fendalton, however, started to groan deeply, and to look like a man who had received a terrible blow from fate.

5

Meanwhile,
Back at the Girls' School . . .

Meanwhile, although things were going very well at the school, somehow Miss Taffeta was not satisfied. Perhaps things were going a little too well. A really wicked headmistress likes events to be a shade rough so that she can file her teeth to points against them. Miss Taffeta's was not an easy nature to satisfy. And the girls were far from contented.

The lessons were not good but they could have put up with that. What worried them most was the terrible food. They all complained, and none more so than three particularly dashing girls in the fourth form, one tall, one small, one full of curiosity, and all three clever.

"Everything's so lumpy," exclaimed Sabella Partridge, the tall one. "There are grey lumps in the porridge, green lumps in the soup, pink lumps in the sausage, and as for the pudding . . .!"

"The porridge is too thin and the soup too fat," cried little Gamble McPhee, "and as for the pudding . . .!"

"The sausages are too old and the potatoes too young," declared Faustine Smith-Smith, a girl so alert with scientific curiosity she even looked like a charming fox-terrier. "And as for the pudding . . .!"

The pudding was called Bran Surprise, and there was more bran than surprise about it, though it had to be admitted there were a few surprises, and all of them nasty. Several girls had written tear-stained letters asking to be brought home, and all on account of the Bran Surprise. However, their parents, reading the letters at breakfast, while supping mango juice and eating delicious pancakes dripping with peach-and-brandy syrup, all agreed that what their daughters needed was plain, hard living in case they became spoiled. Being rich, they were worried that their daughters might grow up spoiled, whereas the girls, being younger and less experienced, did not worry about this at all.

The only pupil who steadily ate her way through everything that she could get was Phoebe Clackett, whose father was a lieutenant-colonel. Phoebe's eating record was so good

that she was given top marks in every subject and was made head prefect into the bargain.

"Eating is part of life," Miss Taffeta said, wearing her grey wig and a benevolent expression at morning assembly. "I want you to learn by Phoebe's example. It is not enough to be beautiful like Sabella, or humorous like Gamble, or scientific like Faustine. You must learn to eat the nutritious food prepared for you by Mrs. Wheatley, and learn to be well-rounded personalities."

"You're certainly coining money," Bainbridge said admiringly to his sister as they sat over coffee and liqueurs, one evening, in their luxurious sitting room on the top floor. Miss Taffeta was marking science tests with one hand and counting her ill-gotten profits with the other.

"Yes, I know," she said in a discontented voice. "I can't think why I'm not happier about it. Could it be that money does not bring happiness? Surely not! And Bainbridge, I hope you checked on that boiler before you came up. If this school explodes it must be because I choose to explode it, and not because of some bent valve."

But Bainbridge had come upon an interesting item in the *Circus Performer's Gazette*, a magazine he still subscribed to even though he hadn't been a circus performer for years.

"Tatiana, listen to this," he cried. "RUINED!'

says the headline in large type. 'Mr Fendalton
Bassett, the philosopher-farmer, woke this
morning to find his fields of sugarbeet covered
with caramel custard as a result of a freak volcanic eruption. "I am ruined, ruined!" sobbed
Mr Bassett bitterly.' Isn't that interesting?"
Bainbridge asked, looking over at his sister who
stared back at him as if he had given her an

unexpected present.

"Bainbridge, for once in your life you may have justified your existence," she declared. "There are great possibilities in that news item, and tomorrow morning I shall check them out, you may be sure of that."

And she returned to marking the science tests with a new enthusiasm.

[6]

A Fascinating Telephone Call

"Ruined! I am ruined!" cried Fendalton. "My farm is feet deep in a fatal flood of caramel custard. I am insured against flood, fire, drought, damage by hail, earthquakes, locusts, nuclear attack, possums and giant moles, but I did not take out a policy against custard. It's a million to one chance, I thought, and I didn't insure against it. I'm ruined." He sobbed broken-heartedly, pausing only to dip his toast in his tea to soften the crust.

"It's quite a nice custard – the taste, that is," said Tancred, "though it is very lumpy. I'll go and get a bucketful, pick the lumps out and we'll have it for lunch with fresh fruit salad. We might as well get some pleasure out of it."

He left Fendalton, whose lamentations, though understandable, were becoming hard to bear, and hurried off with a bucket and a trowel to the mountain of caramel custard, beautifully gilded by the early morning sun.

This was an unfortunate move for no sooner
had he left than the telephone rang, and
Fendalton, forgetting that he was not supposed
to answer it, promptly picked up the receiver,
still sobbing broken-heartedly.

"Fendalton Bassett speaking," he said.

"Hello," said a husky voice with a fascinating
foreign accent he could not quite place. "You are

the man with the mountain of custard?"

Fendalton quivered as if he had been shot. He instantly adored, sight unseen, the owner of this mysterious, melancholy voice.

"I do own a large custard," he agreed, "but don't let's talk about custard. I would rather talk about you."

"But you do not understand . . ." said the husky voice. "I wish to buy a sample of your custard. I am willing to pay ten cents a square metre."

Fendalton shot a distracted glance out of the

window. The custard was so large that ten cents a metre would amount to a small fortune.

"I would be very happy to discuss the matter with you," he said.

"Good. I will come with my front end-loader and tiled trailer tonight. I'll be there at midnight."

"Wonderful," gasped Fendalton.

"You may think it strange that I choose to come at such a late hour," the voice continued, "but I find it a good hour for business deals, because it is dark and quiet and easy to concentrate."

"It's just what I feel." Fendalton cried. "We obviously have a lot in common. Would a glass of home-made sparkling parsnip champagne assist you to concentrate?"

"I find champagne at midnight a great aid to concentration," the voice said in silky tones. "I am already looking forward to meeting you more than I can say."

The telephone clicked as she hung up. Fendalton lay grasping the receiver for a little longer. He thought he could smell perfume down the line. Then he leaped up and reeled across the room to put his head under the cold tap. Weeks had passed since he was last in love and now it came as a great shock to his system.

A few miles away Miss Taffeta sat staring at the telephone with a triumphant smile.

"Bingo!" she said. "It's bingo, Bainbridge! Wickedness wins again!"

[7]

The Lady on the Front-end Loader

The moment Tancred came back into the room he knew that somehow or other Fendalton had managed to fall in love again. For one thing, he was whistling and looking silly. As Tancred watched him he began to gaze earnestly into the mirror, trying to cover his bald patch with special locks of hair he had grown for this very purpose.

At the school, Sabella, Gamble and Faustine were watching Bainbridge with considerable surprise.

"Wetwax is jacking up the swimming pool," said Sabella.

"He's putting it on wheels," Gamble observed. "He's turning it into a sort of giant trailer."

"But who'd want a trailer as big as that?" asked Faustine. "And what would they put in it? And how would they pull it along?"

They had no answers to any of these questions, and at quarter to twelve that night they were asleep and did not see Miss Taffeta set forth on her custard quest.

In her pink-lined boudoir where she kept her most secret cupboards and her most private desk, Miss Taffeta put on her false eyelashes and splashed herself with expensive perfume. She dressed in a very slinky frock, black silk stockings and high heels. Then she put a gold chain with a heart on it around her right ankle and pinned a red rose to her bosom. A few moments later she was driving off in the school's front-end loader, with the school swimming pool – now converted into a trailer – lumbering behind her.

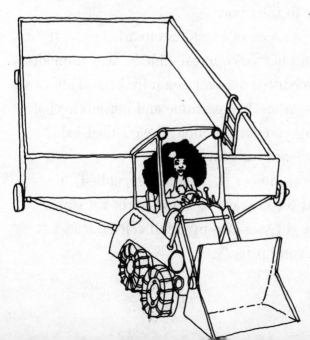

Tucked into his bed Fendalton pretended to be asleep hoping to trick Tancred, and Tancred pretended to be asleep hoping to trick Fendalton. They lay breathing evenly and deeply in the soft, custard-smelling night. Over a nearby chair was Fendalton's Chinese dressing-gown, while his elegant cigarette-holder lay on the dressing-table beside his hair brush. The moment he heard the front-end loader turning into his gate, Fendalton leaped out of bed, put on his dressing-gown, brushed his hair yet again, fitted a cigarette into the silver holder with trembling fingers, ran to the refrigerator to get the parsnip champagne, and then strolled casually to the door.

What a scene of loveliness met his eyes. If he had found her voice irresistible he was immediately enchanted all over again by Miss Taffeta's false eyelashes, her perfume and her ankle chain.

"I rang you earlier about the custard," she said. "Do you have any left?"

"Several tons of it," Fendalton replied. "I resented the custard to begin with, yet since it has brought you into my life I regard it as a pearl beyond price."

"Oh, surely not!" Miss Taffeta sounded worried for a moment. "I am not rich . . . Dear sir, ten cents per square metre is the absolute utmost I can pay."

"Don't let's spoil this beautiful moonlit hour with sordid commerce," quavered Fendalton. "May I pour you a glass of parsnip champagne?"

His hand shook so much as he poured that the parsnip champagne trembled in the glass, seeming to send out showers of silver sparks and little rainbows. There they stood in the moonlight, little knowing that Tancred, watching them, was thinking that Miss Taffeta's back looked unreliable. He decided to take a close look at the front-end loader and the tiled trailer. So bright was the moonlight he was able to make out a plate set into the side of the trailer that said, *This portable swimming pool is the property of Forest Glades School for Girls.* A moment later he nearly became the first boy ever to have been run over by a swimming pool, for Miss Taffeta had started the front-end loader and was moving towards the mountain of custard. Tancred watched with grudging admiration as she simultaneously toasted Fendalton with a glass of his own parsnip champagne and used the front-end loader to fill the swimming pool with big dollops of custard. He watched as Fendalton, anxious to lavish gifts upon this exotic beauty, gave Miss Taffeta a couple of bottles of parsnip champagne to take home with her.

"Very strange," said Tancred to himself, watching as she drove the front-end loader and swimming pool out into the shadows of the road beyond the farm. "How do I find out about this woman? And what can she want with all that custard?"

Back at the school Miss Taffeta put the swimming pool into its hold, the front-end loader into the shed and, not liking to waste anything, the two bottles of parsnip champagne in the science cupboard next to powerful chemicals like hydrochloric acid and trinitrotoluene.

That seemed the proper place for it.

[8]

A Change in Diet

The next day the girls of Forest Glades School woke to find the swimming pool had been placed out of bounds.

"There is a fault in the filter system," said Miss Taffeta at assembly, "but to make up for your disappointment at not being able to swim, there is an extra special breakfast."

The breakfast was caramel custard. They were all quite pleased as it tasted so much nicer than the usual porridge.

"But even this is lumpy!" murmured Sabella, idly picking out some of the lumps with her spoon. All around the table other girls were doing likewise.

"Three sorts of lumps," agreed little Gamble. "Soft, crunchy and hard."

"But look at Phoebe eating it!" Faustine exclaimed.

Lumps or not, the head prefect was devouring

enormous quantities of custard and for once Mrs Wheatley, the cook, was dealing it out with a liberal hand. You would have thought she had access to an unlimited supply.

Sabella scraped the custard off one lump and looked at it carefully.

"It looks just like pumice," she exclaimed, but without excitement, for she was one of those tall, languid girls who never get fussed about anything.

"This one is a sort of blue clay," commented Gamble. "Still, it's better than some of the things we used to find in Bran Surprise."

"This one seems like glass." Faustine sounded deeply puzzled. "Look, we've got to collect the dishes after breakfast. Let's save all the lumps and I'll do a few tests on them later." Faustine was very interested in all aspects of science.

For lunch there was caramel custard, and then for dinner it was caramel custard again. It was during this meal that Phoebe Clackett began to complain of not feeling well. She said she felt light-headed.

"Nonsense!" said Matron Casubon (for Mrs Wheatley, the cook, had hastily run to get the matron). "Pull yourself together!"

"There's so much of her that pulling herself together would take a week," said Gamble to the others. As it was, poor Phoebe did not try. She simply grew paler and paler and complained more and more loudly until at last

Matron Casubon was forced to ring the Fergusson Clinic, who sent around their own ambulance, two stretcher-bearers, and their best doctor, Dr Vashti, a very pleasant woman.

"It looks a lot like pumice poisoning," she said at last. "These cases are very rare, for not many people eat a lot of pumice in this area. I shall take her to the Fergusson clinic for tests and a few painless experiments."

"But she is head prefect. I need her," cried Miss Taffeta, forgetting for the moment she was taking the part of Matron Casubon. However, nobody noticed and in her brief confusion she let them carry Phoebe off on the mink-lined stretcher the clinic kept especially for wealthy patients.

[9]

A Rare Disease of the Well-to-do

Just before lunch was due to be served, Dr Vashti telephoned from the Fergusson Clinic sounding extremely happy.

"Miss Taffeta," she said. "I must congratulate you. Phoebe Clackett is suffering from a very rare illness. At first it seemed like mere pumice poisoning, and indeed there was a lot of pumice in her system, but our special tests have shown that she is actually afflicted with diamond poisoning. She shows a very high hardness index and refracts light. Shine a light in one eye and a rainbow comes out of an ear . . . It is quite remarkable. We are sending our inspectors round to check on your catering arrangements."

"Oh, very well," said Miss Taffeta making an impatient note to fill the larder from her own larder and deep freeze with turkey, sucking pig, pineapples, oranges and chocolate mousse. "But do bear in mind, Doctor, that this is an establishment specially intended for daughters of the rich. They expect nothing but the best and that is what we try to provide."

"You may have been overdoing it," Dr Vashti replied. "Our inspectors are due to examine a large volcanic custard in your area and they will call in on your school on the way home.

"Bainbridge!" hissed Miss Taffeta as she slammed down the receiver. "That farmer along the road has a fortune in diamonds hidden in his custard. I must marry him at once and get possession of the entire property. You shall be our best man."

"All right," said Bainbridge who had been best man at many of her previous marriages. He didn't mind being best man but he couldn't help sighing and wishing for simpler times. Given the choice he much preferred being a dancing gorilla.

At that very moment, in the science room, Faustine looked at Sabella and Gamble in utter amazement. Before her were the stones collected from the breakfast and lunch plates – seventy lumps of pumice, fifty lumps of blue clay, all inscribed with teeth marks, as well as a hundred and twenty walnut-sized stones which seemed to interest Faustine particularly.

"They're diamonds!" she exclaimed. "Fifty-two blue-white diamonds, thirty-eight ice-white, twenty-two silver cape, and eight blue ones." She had an old jeweller's glass of her father's screwed in one eye. "And all found in our custard!"

"I thought it was rich custard," Gamble said with a giggle. "Let's put on our togs this evening, go out to the pool and see if we can find any more. It's time we had some fun around here, and diamonds promise fun of the highest standard."

[10]

Tancred Has Further Fears for Fendalton

Meanwhile Fendalton sat staring at the telephone. Dust gathered on the covers of his philosophy books.

"Suppose she does not ring again," he exclaimed. "She came out of nowhere and vanished back into it. She left no address." He gazed hungrily at the telephone which obligingly rang at that exact moment. Fendalton seized it as a starving man might grasp at a proffered banana.

"My darling," said a husky voice. "You have been much on my mind. I shall come to visit you again at midnight. And how is the custard surviving the warm weather?"

"Very well, thank you," babbled Fendalton. "It's standing up to it very well." When he put the receiver down he smiled radiantly at Tancred.

"Oh joy!" he cried. "She loves me!"

"Big deal!" said Tancred. "Remember what happened last time."

"Don't mention that occasion in the same breath," exclaimed Fendalton, shuddering. "This is the first time I have ever really and truly been in love. The rest were mere boyish infatua-

tions. Now I'll put some more parsnip champagne on ice and then I'll gather some flowers."

Off he went, singing and skipping. Tancred took the champagne out of the refrigerator when he wasn't looking, carried it out and poured it into the custard which immediately began to respond to the rare old vintage by bubbling in a particularly threatening way. Great yellow bubbles swelled deep in the custard and, rising to the surface, broke with sullen plops. The whole surface of the custard began to seethe. Tancred stared at it uneasily for several minutes before going to fill the empty bottles with harmless ginger beer, put the corks in once more and even wired them down again, and covered them with the original gold paper.

"If Fendalton really loves her and she loves him I mustn't stand in their way," he said reasonably enough, "but how can I make sure? Suppose she is some vampire or adventuress? Well, at least he isn't likely to get married and make a will in her favour."

For, strangely enough, though Fendalton fell in love with atrocious ease, and had once been engaged to five women at the same time, the mere mention of matrimony terrified him and caused him to fall out of love immediately.

The day passed slowly with Fendalton singing and skipping around. Tancred sat moodily reading *The Poultry and Sugarbeet Farmer's Press* which had just been delivered. An item of gossip under the heading Social Chit Chat caught his eye.

'Prominent among the many glamorous patients at the Fergusson Clinic yesterday was Phoebe, lovely daughter of Lieutenant-Colonel and Mrs Clackett. Mrs Clackett was one of the Miss Gummidges prior to her marriage. Close secrecy surrounds Phoebe's hospitalization, but a little bird tells me that her complaint is one available only to the upper classes. Phoebe is head prefect at Forest Glades School for Girls.'

Tancred stared at this item. "Forest Glades," he murmured to himself. "If I could get in there for a night I could find out more about Uncle Fendalton's midnight visitor." He thought about this deeply for some time.

[11]

A New Head Prefect for Forest Glades School for Girls

The sound of suggestive cabaret songs filled the air as Miss Taffeta, in her capacity as Madame le Sage, corrected French translation. She had spent her lunch hour searching through her blackmailing books for a clergyman with a guilty past, but there are not as many of them as you might think. Of the mere dozen or so she did find, many of them had given up the Church and gone in for television, or lived so far away it was difficult to contact them about an immediate wedding ceremony. However, she had located a very promising man, and smiled as she dealt contemptuously with the work the girls had passed in. Suddenly the walkie-talkie gave a snarl and then spoke in a resentful voice.

"Bainbridge calling Tatiana! Bainbridge calling Tatiana!"

"I read you loud and clear, Bainbridge," said

Miss Taffeta briskly. "Come in, Bainbridge! Are you speaking as Wetwax or Scroggins?"

"I'm Wetwax, aren't I?" cried Bainbridge crossly. "Listen, I'm not too happy about this boiler. You'll have to get a genuine mechanic to look at it."

"Pull yourself together, Bainbridge!" commanded Miss Taffeta. "I'm worn out with locating a clergyman. I'll need to have a bit of a breather before I start looking for a mechanic I can blackmail."

"Pay him," suggested Bainbridge. "Play it straight."

"Don't be ridiculous," snapped his sister. "Over and out."

"No – hang on!" Bainbridge shouted. "There's a girl here who says she's a wandering head prefect looking for relief work. Shall I send her up?"

"Oh yes, do!" Miss Taffeta was delighted.

Ten minutes later Miss Taffeta had changed a tape of French songs for some Mozart. She had also put on her grey wig, and was interviewing a tall, freckled girl who said her name was Greta Bassett. She wore a rather old-fashioned

school uniform with a huge prefect's badge on it. *Greta Bassett – Head Prefect*, proclaimed the badge.

"Bassett! Bassett! Where have I heard that name?" pondered Miss Taffeta. "Oh well, no doubt there are many Bassetts, one way and another. And why did you leave your last school?"

"They said I was too strict with the girls," Greta Bassett replied, her eyes darting curiously around the study. "But I like being strict. If one can't be strict with others there's not much point in being a prefect, is there?"

"My own sentiments. I am in favour of strictness and even six of the best should the occasion demand it," said Miss Taffeta. If she had had a heart it would have warmed towards Greta Bassett. "Now for another question of great importance. Do you have a good appetite?" Greta Bassett hesitated.

"I eat a lot if I can get it," she said, and added cunningly, "I am particularly fond of custard."

Miss Taffeta's eyes shone.

"Good, good," she exclaimed, "but life is not all custard! What is your attitude to bran?"

"I know it is good for me," said Greta Bassett without hesitation.

"Splendid!" cried Miss Taffeta. "Well, take your suitcase to the first floor (I'm afraid the lift is rather slow but you'll get there eventually) and sign on with Matron Casubon who will show you your bed in the dormitory."

"The dormitory!" exclaimed Greta Bassett, unexpectedly taken aback.

"Oh yes!" said Miss Taffeta, "I think a head

prefect should share a dormitory with the rest of the girls. It gives plenty of opportunity to be strict."

Greta Bassett left the room blushing deeply.

"What a sweet, old-fashioned girl," pondered Miss Taffeta, changing into the wig, smock and cap of Matron Casubon as she swung deftly down the fire-escape. "But why should that name Bassett ring such a ding-dong bell? Well, never mind . . . I need a head prefect until Phoebe returns. Even when I marry Fendalton and get a large fortune in diamonds I may well keep the school going just as a profitable hobby."

She laughed wickedly, but the sound was smothered by the ivy which grew so thickly over the mellow brick walls of the school.

[12]

Fendalton Waits

Fendalton was busy, for officials of the Health Department had come out from the Fergusson Clinic. They seethed like ants around the edge of his giant custard, putting pieces of it into test tubes and sealing them, heating it, freezing it, dipping litmus paper into it, applying iodine, sodium hydroxide, whipped cream, stewed plums, and other suitable chemicals.

"The molecules of this custard are very complex," said the official with the microscope. "It will be most interesting to see just what happens when we pass electricity through it. Meanwhile it would be most inadvisable for you to think of electrocuting it yourself. Keep it quiet and inert and all will be well. We will come back tomorrow with our own generator and batteries and copper wire.. . that is, if it stays fine. It does look as it if might rain."

Fendalton glanced anxiously at an inky sky

over the distant hills, and imagined his beloved
driving towards him through the rain, her frail
form in the front-end loader battered by the
storm. As he stared, an ominous bolt of lightning struck across the blue-black, bulging
clouds lolloping up from behind the hills.
Fendalton groaned softly, and for a moment it
seemed to him that the custard quivered with
sympathy and apprehension.

58

[13]

Up and Down the Fire-escapes at Forest Glades

Night fell – a mottled, cloudy night of occasional stars and frequent clouds. Every now and then the thunder crashed like giant saucepans falling out of an untidy kitchen cupboard.

At 10.30 pm Miss Taffeta, heavily scented and eye-lashed, set off in her red racing car. She wanted more than a mere swimming pool full of custard this time. She was playing for big stakes. How anxiously she had watched as the Health Department officials tested the custard in the swimming pool with their various chemicals, but they had not been interested in the lumps, only in the custard itself. Luck was with her. However, as she passed the boiler room she heard a thumping noise as if a prisoner, bound and gagged inside it, was trying desperately to break his way out by hitting the door with his feet. She immediately stopped her car and took out her walkie-talkie.

"Tatiana calling Bainbridge. Tatiana calling Bainbridge. Come in, Bainbridge." And then when Bainbridge did come in, she shouted rudely, "Bainbridge, get off your fat bottom and come here at once. The boiler's playing up again. Fix it, and meet me in an hour and a half at the farm down the road. I'll need you to be my best man and my witness, too. I'm just off to pick up the clergyman." Then she accelerated furiously, and drove off in a shower of dust and gravel.

Bambridge sighed. He had just put on his gorilla suit. The curious thing was that, as a man, he was nothing much to look at, but as a gorilla he was magnificent. He couldn't resist going down to the boiler room wearing his suit, for it was warm and cosy, and the night looked particularly threatening.

As the racing car left the school grounds Sabella, Gamble and Faustine, who had been keeping watch from the dormitory window, climbed down one of the many fire-escapes. They were careful not to attract the attention of the new head prefect at the other end of the dormitory. It was not difficult to do this as the head prefect had put her head into the pillow-case and then covered herself with the bed quilt. She seemed remarkably shy for a head prefect.

The girls climbed in at the window of the science room where Faustine collected assorted batteries, chemicals, microscopes, coils of copper wire and all the equipment necessary for testing lumpy custard. Then they made off to the swimming pool, Sabella still languid, Gamble making jokes and giggling at them, and Faustine looking keen and clever.

Shortly after they had vanished the new head prefect took her head out of the pillow-case and looked around furtively.

Tancred – for of course it was he, disguised in his mother's old school uniform and prefect's badge – made for the window and climbed out of it. However, he went up the fire-escape, not down. Once, glancing into the school grounds below him, he got a nasty shock for he thought he saw a large gorilla wandering by with a tool kit in one paw. But the grounds were full of deceptive shadows and he realized he must have been mistaken.

"Don't let your imagination run away with you," he told himself, as he climbed through the window of Miss Taffeta's boudoir with all the determination of a boy anxious to save a well-loved uncle from the effects of a serious weakness over which he had no control.

[14]

A Disastrous Midnight Assignation

At about five minutes to midnight Fendalton
heard the spin of wheels and hastened out to
greet Miss Taffeta.

He had laid the table with flowers and can-
dles, and had even found an ice bucket for the
parsnip champagne. Then he had brushed his
hair over his bald spot, and put on a plum-
coloured velvet jacket. These preparations had
taken up so much of his time that he had barely
noticed Tancred was missing, though when he
thought about it he couldn't help being pleased
that the boy was keeping himself busy and
above all, out of the way.

Yet now, by the intermittent flashes of lightning, he could see that Miss Taffeta was not
alone. She was assisting a very seedy-looking
passenger out of the car – a clergyman,
Fendalton thought, though it was hard to tell to
which church he belonged. He wore an ordinary

clergyman's collar and coat, yet carried a small idol in one hand, and with the other led a black goat on a string.

"What can this mean?" Fendalton muttered to himself uneasily, as he held the door wide to let them in.

"My darling," he cried tenderly.

"My little custard king," she answered, wrapping him in an embrace so scorching that the

lapels of his velvet jacket began to smoke slightly. "The hours of our separation have crept by
like drowsy snails. Let us never part again. Look,
I have brought a clergyman, the Reverend Cecil
Scowbottom, and as soon as my brother gets
here – which he had better do soon or I'll cut his
ears off – we can be united in holy matrimony."

The goat began to eat one of the sofa cushions,
and Miss Taffeta fluttered her eyelashes at
Fendalton so very vigorously that all the petals
on the rose in his buttonhole blew away.
Fendalton did not flutter back. Within two sec-
onds flat he had fallen out of love. His infatuation
for Miss Taffeta was utterly over and done with.

"Marriage!" he said in a desperate voice. "But I
must have time to think this over."

"Do not trifle with my affections," she cried in
steely tones.

"No, no! Nothing is further from my thoughts,"
Fendalton said with increasing alarm. "But I can-
not allow you to sacrifice yourself like this. It is
nothing but a girlish infatuation. Go your way,
fancy-free, and I will try to recover from a bro-
ken heart."

"Take all the time you want," said Miss Taffeta

sweetly, "provided you make up your mind by the time my brother Bambridge gets here. Think carefully, for it is a big decision."

With these words she produced a gun – her Colt *Peacemaker* – and pointed it at him. "I will do all I can to help you make up your mind."

The rain roared down and the goat began nibbling another cushion. At this moment the custard became convulsed and writhed luminously. It had been struck by lightning!

[15]

Up in the Boudoir

Up in Miss Taffeta's boudoir Tancred drew a deep breath. There were many cupboards and a big desk, unusual in a room draped with pink silk, lit by fringed lampshades. He was sure he would find clues to her true nature in this private room. Opening the wardrobe door he leaped back with a yell of terror, for it seemed to be filled with hanged women. Half-a-dozen suspended figures moved as the door opened. Tancred felt as if a fmger of ice were running up and down his spine. A moment later he saw that what he had taken for figures were nothing more than a set of wigs, with matching clothes suspended beneath them. He recognized the cap and uniform and wig belonging to Matron Casubon, and the severe geometrical suit belonging to Mrs Function, the maths teacher.

"Aha!" he said triumphantly. "I'm on the right track."

A search of the bookcase showed that what appeared to be a volume of Shakespeare's plays was actually a box containing fine whisky, and that the novels of Sir Walter Scott, handsomely bound in green and gold, were back copies of *The Blackmailer's Diary and Account Book* going back over the past ten years

"So!" Tancred muttered. "Now we know where we are."

But he didn't, quite!

In the bottom drawer of Miss Taffeta's desk he came on a lot of old circus programmes.

"Gloria and Her Dancing Gorilla", he read. "Consuela, the Human Cannonball". The photographs were those of Miss Taffeta herself. He couldn't help admiring her, but it was plain she was not a woman who would make his Uncle Fendalton a restful wife. Under the programme were a pile of disturbing documents – blank marriage licences, death certificates fastened together with a bulldog clip, false passports, and so on.

Through a window the lightning snapped a quick, white smile at him and thunder drummed furiously all around the sky. Tancred caught a glimpse of a curious little flicker on the window pane, not quite lightning, although it came and went quickly. He looked across the playground below and saw something which intrigued him. People with torches and umbrellas were working in the swimming pool. While his first plan was to climb on his bike and pedal back to the farm to confront Fendalton with the evidence he had concerning Miss Taffeta, he couldn't help being inquisitive about the swimming pool incident. Was it one of the girlish pranks that take place in school stories, or was it some custard activity he ought to know about? After all, until Phoebe was cured of her select disease, he was actually head prefect of Forest Glades School for Girls, and he didn't like to betray his mother's fine tradition. Quickly he folded up a few death and marriage certificates, slipping them into his dressing-gown pocket. Then he started off down the fire-escape and made for the glimmering, whispering swimming pool full of custard and secrets.

[16]

Custard Electrification and its Consequences

Down in the swimming pool Sabella and Gamble sported in the custard wearing glamorous swimming togs and sieving the custard for any diamonds it might contain, while Faustine prepared her experiments on it using a variety of school chemicals.

"What on earth is this?" she cried, shining the torch on the lable of a green bottle with a gold top. "One bottle of Pars. Champ. I've never heard of Pars. Champ. before." She opened the bottle which popped in a festive way and foamed out into the custard.

"It smells like some sort of wine," she said in great puzzlement, dipping a litmus paper into it. The litmus paper turned such a bright red it glowed in the dark. "It must be very acid. I might as well pour it away. The Department of Health people put a lot of chemicals into this

custard so a bottle of Pars. Champ. won't make much difference."

"I think we've collected all the biggest stones," Gamble called. "I haven't found one for ages. But how on earth does a caramel custard come to be full of diamonds?"

"It's very strange," Faustine said. "This custard must be of volcanic origin – formed under great pressure, with a bit of atmospheric oxygen thrown in. I can't explain it. All right! You must get out now because I'm going to pass an electric current through the custard. There are some very strange molecules and I want to see how they react to an electrical surprise."

"Yes, out you get," said a new voice and, looking up, they beheld the head prefect illuminated in the ghastly glow of lightning reflecting off a swimming pool full of custard. "You're not supposed to be swimming at this time of night, and particularly not in custard."

"We are conducting a scientific experiment," Faustine said calmly, "and it can only be conducted during a thunderstorm. Do you see what I have here?"

"It looks like a kite," said the head prefect in an interested voice. "Gosh, it's a good one, isn't it? Did you make it?"

"I certainly did," said Faustine. "Now watch me! Putting on rubber gloves and gumboots, I carefully pull the string out, then I tie the string to this battery. Then I watch this dial. I don't know what will happen if . . . ah, did you see that?"

Lightning struck the kite, ran down the string and caused the needle on the dial to take a great leap. The custard blazed out, iridescent with the force of the naked electricity roaring through it.

"Hold the torch," Faustine said to Gamble, who was standing watching, dripping custard everywhere.

"But where did you get this?" asked the head

prefect, picking up a bottle, apparently amazed. "It's parsnip champagne. How on earth did it come to be here?"

"How did *you* come to be here?" Gamble asked. "That's a greater mystery. Did you follow us?"

But within the next moment they had stopped wondering anything at all. There was a thick gurgling sound and the whole custard began to gyrate, turning in a spiral as if it were about to flow out of a plug hole in the bottom of the swimming pool.

"Can the parsnip champagne have eaten a hole through solid concrete?" speculated Faustine in some excitement, but the words ended in a gasp as the custard suddenly flowed to one end of the swimming pool, and then reared up like a cross

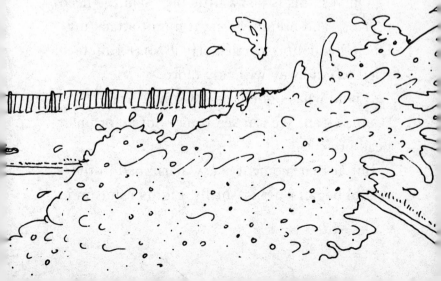

between a cobra and a jellyfish, not a pretty sight late on a stormy night. The next moment it formed itself an arm and struck a blow at the swimming pool fence, then somehow sucked itself up, and over, and out, flooding towards the gate in a yellow blobbly fashion.

"Follow it!" hissed Faustine.

"In our swimming togs?" asked Sabella, who was not very keen on pursuing an active caramel custard through the night. "Let it go!"

"We've got the diamonds," said Gamble, always practical.

"I must follow it," said the head prefect. "I think it's trying to get back home to join up with the rest of itself."

"You mean there's more of it?" cried Faustine.

"Oh yes, this is just a little bit," said the head prefect, "and not only that, it might attack my Uncle Fendalton, particularly if Miss Taffeta tried to get away with any more."

"Look, what's going on?" Gamble asked. "Come clean. We can see you're not an ordinary head prefect."

But at that moment every alarm bell in the school began ringing shrilly. Lights came on in the dormitory windows, and girls began to scramble down the fire-escape.

"Have they found out that we're missing?" Gamble asked, bewildered.

"No!" said Sabella, slightly less languid than usual. "Look, the whole school is trembling. Surely it can't be the effect of the custard."

"What is that curious thudding sound?" Faustine frowned. "It sounds like – oh, I don't know what it sounds like, but it sounds dangerous."

The next moment the front of the school garage burst open, and out roared the front-end loader driven by a frantic gorilla.

"Run! Run!" it shrieked. "Get Tatiana! The boiler valve is permanently stuck and it's going to blow up at any moment."

"Walking custard, and gorillas driving front-end loaders!" exclaimed the head prefect. "I'm sure my mother never, ever had to put up with anything like this when she was head prefect. Where's my bike? I must be off and warn Fendalton!"

[17]

A Confusing Evening

Down on the farm Fendalton stared at Miss Taffeta.

"Don't you kid yourself, baby!" said Miss Taffeta. "It's going to be all right! I'll be your wife first and you'd better watch it, or I'll be your widow directly, unless, of course, you agree to give me the custard as a wedding present."

"You are too impetuous," cried Fendalton desperately. "Reflect a mere moment! You'll be throwing yourself away on a penniless man. My farm is currently covered in custard and I can claim no insurance."

"Insurance! Pig's bum!" said Miss Taffeta coarsely. "That custard is full of diamonds."

"Diamonds!" shouted Fendalton.

"Diamonds?" wheezed the Reverend Scowbottom, and looked out of the window in the general direction of the electrified custard. His face changed shape with sudden terror.

"Look! Look!" he shouted.

"What, and let you try to get my gun off me?" chuckled Miss Taffeta. "I didn't come down in the last shower of rain, Sunshine."

"But the custard is on the march!" screamed the agitated clergyman. "It's a sign to the ungodly. I repent! I repent! I will never sacrifice another goat after this." He rolled on the floor in a state of such sincerity that Fendalton, and

even Miss Taffeta, decided to sneak a quick look out of the window. But the goat yawned and began to eat Fendalton's umbrella.

Imagine their feelings when by the light of almost continuous flashes of lightning they could see the whole mountain of custard advancing furiously towards them. Freckled with pumice and bubbling all over, it actually managed to sparkle a little too, whenever the lightning picked out a diamond embedded in it. There was something about its vile, oozing approach that would have struck terror into the sternest heart and should have caused a weak woman to falter. Miss Taffeta, however, enjoyed danger. She grabbed a spare clip of ammunition and went out on to the verandah.

"Don't irritate it. Try to reason with it.

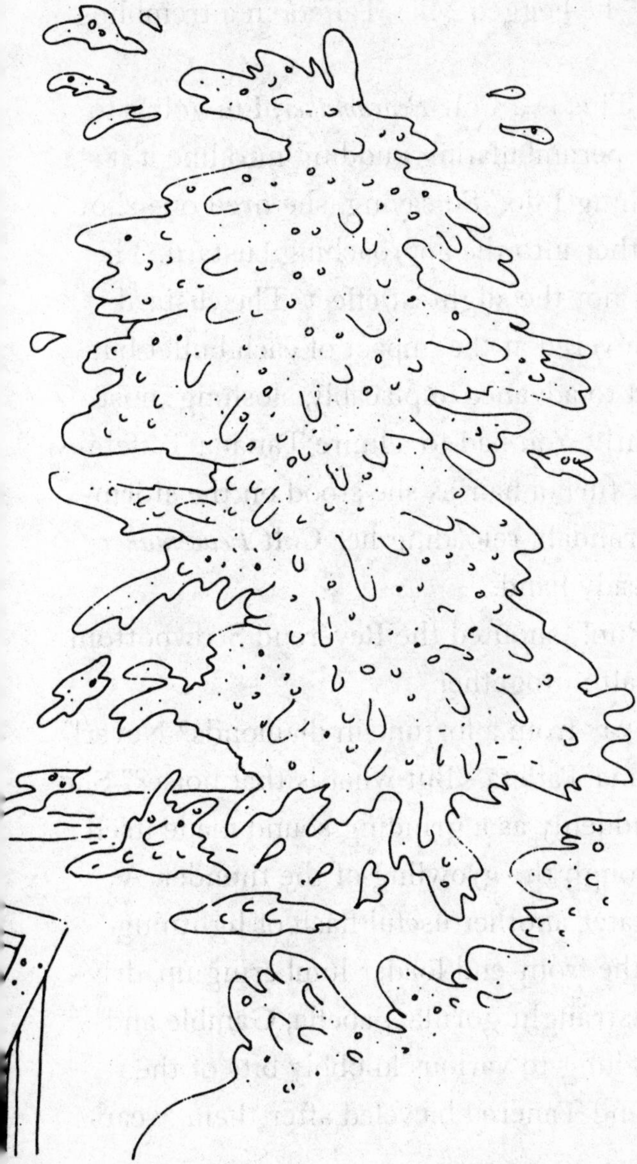

Humour it," shouted Fendalton. "Be careful with that gun!" he begged Miss Taffeta in a trembling voice.

"Gun? This is a Colt *Peacemaker*. I'm going to bring the perambulating pudding into line if it's the last thing I do." So saying, she fired one shot after another into the approaching custard. The shots had not the slightest effect. The custard merely quivered at the impact of each bullet but continued to advance implacably, sloshing most unpleasantly. You had to admire Tatiana Taffeta — she didn't turn a hair as she stood on the storm-lashed verandah, reloading her Colt *Peacemaker* with a steady hand.

"Run! Run!" shouted the Reverend Scowbottom and Fendalton together.

"Run away from a fortune in diamonds? Never!" said Tatiana Taffeta. "But what is that noise?" She turned suddenly as a grinding sound made itself heard through the growling of the thunder. A moment later another useful flash of lightning revealed the front-end loader lumbering up, driven by a distraught gorilla. Sabella, Gamble and Faustine clung to various knobbly bits of the machine and Tancred bicycled after them, wearing his mother's old school uniform and prefect's badge. But this was not all. In front of them, travelling at an impressive speed considering it could only crawl, was a great, flopping piece of caramel custard animated by an identical, unnatural life to that which stirred in the parent custard, causing it to advance on Fendalton's house in an implacable way. As they stared, the smaller custard flung itself against the larger one which immediately came to a standstill.

The thunder roared, but in a more distant voice. The storm was retreating. The two custards slowly flowed back together again then began to move towards the house once more. But now Tancred showed himself in a courageous light. He leaped from his bike and flung himself between the custard and the cottage.

"Back!" he shouted. "Back!"

To everyone's amazement the custard hesitated, and then, as Tancred gesticulated and danced, actually retreated a foot or two.

"Tancred! Don't take any unnecessary risks!" shouted Fendalton, though it was rather late for this good advice.

"Tatiana – the school boiler is about to blow up," cried the gorilla, but even Miss Taffeta was too fascinated by Tancred and the custard to take much notice at first. It began to retreat towards the field of sugarbeet and the volcanic crater in the middle of it.

"What a head prefect!" Miss Taffeta sighed. "I could have done much with her."

"It's a miracle – a blessed miracle," cried the Reverend Scowbottom.

"The swimming-pool custard came alive and we followed it here," Sabella explained to Fendalton. "But why is it doing what he tells it to do?"

"Nature is full of mysteries. We must not seek to know them all," said Fendalton, who didn't have the slightest idea.

"What nonsense," Faustine muttered. "I wish to know every single one of them."

Tancred, meanwhile, had guided the custard to the crater in the middle of the sugarbeet field

and appeared to be talking to it very earnestly, pointing at the crater as he did so. The custard suddenly moved and began to pour over the crater's rim – down, down to the fiery heart of the world, taking a fortune in diamonds with it. It flowed quite smoothly for such a lumpy custard, twinkling occasionally as it vanished. The lightning was not nearly so frequent by now, yet as it flashed once more on the custard, this contrary dessert assumed a wistful beauty as if a yellow carpet, crossed with a golden serpent, were trying to creep out by a back door.

"The boiler! The boiler!" shouted the gorilla, shaking Miss Taffeta by the very arm which held the Colt *Peacemaker*. "Tatiana – the school is about to explode!"

Miss Taffeta reacted with decision. She'd had a crowded evening what with trying to get a black goat into her racing-car, threatening Fendalton, and having a mountain of custard come to life and absorb six shots without so much as wincing. Now she was watching the custard crawl out of everyday life, taking diamonds with it. Yet she snapped into action without a moment's hesitation.

"The school? Explode?" she cried. "Where are my car keys? I must go to the rescue at once."

"It's all right! The girls are safe," panted Bainbridge. Inside the gorilla suit he was think-

ing, "This sort of thing never happens to real gorillas. If I get out of this alive I'll stay a gorilla until the end of my days".

"The girls? The girls? Damn the girls!" yelled wicked Miss Taffeta. "What about my blackmailing diaries, my false passports, my opium, and my disguises? What about my stolen jewellery, my mink coat? Out of my way!" And she rushed from the room though Bainbridge, rather to Fendalton's irritation, tried to stop her.

A moment later her red racing-car screamed out of the farmyard back towards the school, going faster than it had any right to.

"Oh well," said Bainbridge, "it's out of my hands now." He saw them all staring at him and

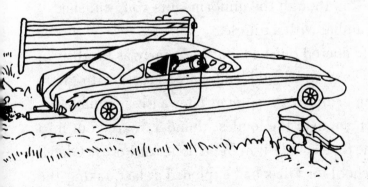

shrugged his shoulders, looking as nonchalant as was possible in the circumstances.

Tancred bounded into the room. The custard was industriously pouring itself into the crater without any need of further guidance.

"Oh, Fendalton! Don't marry her!" he cried. "She has been married fifteen times already."

"Sixteen," said Bainbridge in a resigned voice.

"If I had known *that* it would have been a very different story," Fendalton said, with a bitter smile.

"You're a boy!" said Faustine accusingly to Tancred. "How did you come to be head prefect in a girls' school?"

". . . sleeping in a girls' dormitory . . . said Sabella.

". . . though the uniform suits you," finished Gamble with a giggle.

Tancred blushed, but not nearly as brightly as the sky which suddenly flared across with glowing crimson. A moment later a great rumble, louder than the loudest thunder, roared out into the distracted night. The boiler at Forest Glades School for Girls had exploded at last, taking the whole school, *and* Miss Taffeta, with it.

[18]

Starting All Over Again

On the lawn, outside the farmhouse door, sat
Faustine, Gamble, Sabella and Tancred sorting
their various diamonds and reading aloud from
various newspapers.

"FOREST GLADES SCHOOL FOR GIRLS EXPLODES."

"BURSTING BOILER BLOWS UP LIKE BOMB."

These were but two headlines in the *Poultry and
Sugarbeet Farmers' Press.*

"Educational circles mourn the loss of the
entire staff of Forest Glades School for Girls,"
read Sabella. "All the pupils were saved by the
prompt action of the dedicated old caretaker,
Wetwax, but the teachers, the caretaker, the
butler, the matron and the cook were all
exploded as they attempted to save rare oil
paintings and a Greek antiquity from the
school lift. They have been blown into such
small pieces that all attempts at identification

have proved impossible. There will be a mass
funeral tomorrow conducted by the Reverend
Cecil Scowbottom. The school mascot, a pet
gorilla, is being cared for by Fendalton
Bassett, the farmer-philosopher who is turning his farm into a volcanic park for those
interested in boiling pools, hot mud, and
small volcanoes. It is understood the gorilla is
being trained to conduct people around the

park giving a short lecture on its various attractions. This unique feature should be one enjoyed by many tourists in months to come. The park will be called The Tatiana Taffeta Memorial Park."

"We'll probably never have such an adventurous time again," said Sabella. "All our parents are offering money to help rebuild the school and it is to be called The Tatiana Taffeta Foundation for Enterprising Girls. In a few weeks we'll be back at school eating school sausages once more."

"Lucky we managed to salvage this fortune in diamonds first," said Gamble, "since the custard has vanished into the bowels of the earth."

"How did you manage to stop it?" asked Faustine, looking up at Tancred. "I can't help being puzzled by that."

"Well, I was the one who used to feed the hens, milk the cows and weed the sugarbeet," Tancred explained. "I used to talk to them a bit. Gossip with them, give them the news. Fendalton wasn't much company. And I suddenly thought, Suppose this custard has inherited a respect for my voice? And so it had, you see. I reasoned with it and convinced it it would be happy down in the heart of the world with all the molten iron and lava."

"It was a funny custard to begin with," Faustine said reflectively. "But then it had had a lot of chemicals poured into it, not to mention parsnip champagne, and on top of that it was struck by lightning. That was enough to bring its strange molecules to life."

"It wanted to be reunited with itself," Gamble said. "Lucky for Phoebe Clackett that she had digested all the custard she had eaten, or who knows what might have happened?"

"Tancred!" shouted Fendalton from inside the farm house. "Tancred . . . I must warn you," he said, when Tancred came in. "You are sitting on the lawn with three girls. You are playing with fire. Let an older and wiser man warn you, Tancred . . ."

"It's hard to say which I like best," Tancred said in a dreamy voice. "Sabella has such beautiful, long hair, and I like Gamble's giggle – but then Faustine has a lovely smile and a microscope."

"I will have to watch over you," Fendalton

said gloomily. "You come from an unreliable family. Take these nutritious scraps out to the goat and these sandwiches to the gorilla. He's in the front room watching television."

Out on the lawn the girls, jewellers' glasses screwed into their eyes, went on grading the diamonds in the great pile salvaged from the swimming pool on that memorable night. Everyone looked as if they might live happily ever after.

Meanwhile in a forest several miles distant Miss Taffeta woke up safe and sound on a bed of leaves. She was battered, bruised and penniless, for her entire fortune had been wiped out by the explosion, but she was not downhearted. Being blown up by an exploding school boiler was nothing to a woman who had spent many fruitful hours being fired out of a cannon.

"I will return!" she muttered, wicked as ever. "They haven't heard the last of me. I'll find new jewels to steal, new clergymen to blackmail. I'll ride on more front-end loaders, make more men fall in love with me, set out on midnight businesses again, wearing perfume and false eyelashes. Things were getting too easy to be interesting, anyway. Now the fun has come back into life."

But she did not move right away. Instead, she lay there smiling up through the leaves into the blue air which such a short time ago had been entertaining thunder and lightning and was now bright with sunshine. Then, refreshed by this contact with nature, she polished her Colt *Peacemaker* and set off into the world once more.

About the author

MARGARET MAHY was a librarian for many years before becoming one of the most popular and respected children's writers in the world. She has won the Carnegie Prize several times and every prize that New Zealand can give her national treasures.

Over the years Margaret Mahy has written wonderful books for children at all levels – enchanting picture books, hilarious volumes for younger readers and profound and moving novels for young adults. One of the truly great contemporary writers.

Margaret lives in the South Island of New Zealand with a dog, several cats and a number of other animals and she can always find time to see her children and numerous grandchildren.

Another Barn Owl Book from Margaret Mahy

THE BLOOD AND THUNDER ADVENTURE ON HURRICANE PEAK

One of Margaret Mahy's wonderful, chaotic, zany, fantastic stories. In the great city of Hookywalker lives wicked Sir Quincy Judd-Sprockett in his super modern wheelchair. Sir Quincy is determined to close down the Unexpected School on Hurricane Peak, where young Huxley and Zara Hammond have been sent by their parents. The school is full of unusual characters: Heathcliff Warlock the magical school teacher, Zanzibar the feline head prefect and the amazing inventor, Belladonna Doppler.
Will this unlikely crew manage to foil the fiendish Sir Quincy? Of course they will and loads of fun on the way.